Mystery of the Laughing Dinosaur

THE BOBBSEY TWINS®

MYSTERY OF THE LAUGHING DINOSAUR

Laura Lee Hope

Illustrated by John Speirs

A MINSTREL™ BOOK

PUBLISHED BY POCKET BOOKS NEW YORK

This novel is a work of fiction. Names, characters, places and incidents are either the product of the author's imagination or are used fictitiously. Any resemblance to actual events or locales or persons, living or dead, is entirely coincidental.

 A Minstrel Book, published by
Pocket Books, a division of Simon & Schuster, Inc.,
1230 Avenue of the Americas, New York, N.Y. 10020

Contents

·1·

Dinosaur Antics

Freddie and Bert Bobbsey walked up to the skeleton of a dinosaur that towered over them in the museum hall. Their sisters and their friend, Scott Bishop, lagged behind.

"Look at that!" twelve-year-old Bert exclaimed. "That thing is huge!"

"I'm glad it's not alive," Freddie shuddered. He was only six. "Otherwise, it could eat us up in one gulp!"

Bert strode toward the tail of the dinosaur while Freddie tossed back his blond head and stared at its enormous jaws.

Suddenly, the dinosaur laughed!

Freddie was dumbfounded. "Bert, did you hear that?" he cried. "This creature died more than a million years ago and it still laughs!"

But the dark-haired boy was too fascinated by the powerful tail of the prehistoric animal to pay attention to his brother.

"Bert, listen to me!" Freddie called out again. But a sudden uproar of police sirens and the shout of a museum guard drowned him out.

"Hey, Norman, there's been a robbery!" the guard yelled to his partner, who stood at the other end of the hall. He patted his two-way radio. "I just got the word. A robbery next door."

Freddie gulped. "Bert!" he gasped. "There was a robbery!"

When the older boy did not answer him, Freddie turned to look around. There was no sign of Bert. Freddie started to run to the other side of the

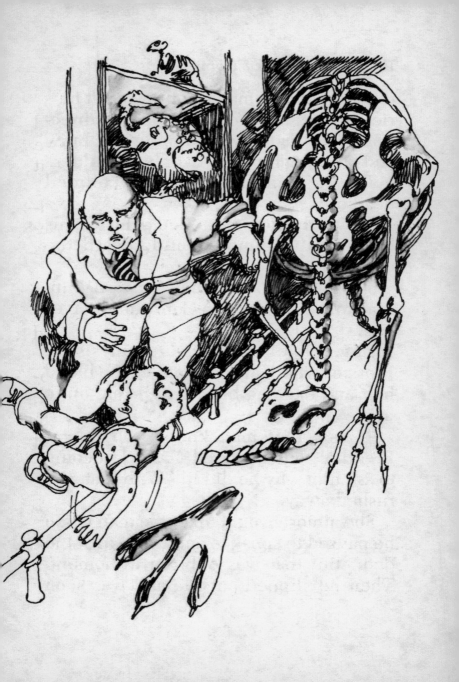

dinosaur as a fat man in a brown suit hurried toward him from the opposite direction. The man was mopping his brow and glancing furtively over his shoulder.

The next moment the two collided head on!

"Ow!" the little boy cried as he lost his balance and tumbled underneath the dinosaur.

The fat man continued forward, running to the entrance on Constitution Avenue.

Immediately Freddie's twin sister, Flossie, who had the same curly, blond hair and dancing blue eyes, came up to him.

"I saw that man knock you down, Freddie!" she declared. "And I'm going to ask him why he did it!" With that, she rushed away.

She almost caught up to the man when he paused to speak to another man at the door. But that was only for a moment. Then he slipped outside and was soon lost in the crowd of people milling around in front of the museum.

Disappointed, Flossie walked back to her brother.

"Where are Nan and Scott?" Freddie asked, still dizzy from his fall, "and Bert?"

"Nan and Scott are coming," Flossie replied and pointed. "But I have no idea where Bert is."

"What happened, Freddie?" Nan, who was Bert's twin, cried out when she reached the younger children. "Are you all right?"

The small boy staggered to his feet. "I-I guess so. You see, the dinosaur laughed and the guard yelled out that there had been a robbery. And then this big, fat man knocked me down."

"What big, fat man?"

"He ran out the door," Flossie said. "Freddie turned to go after Bert and the man ran into him."

Nan brushed her brother's corduroy

pants while her eyes scanned the large room.

"Where *is* Bert?" she asked.

No one knew the answer.

Bert, by now, was in hot pursuit of a redheaded boy. He had noticed the boy crouching behind the dinosaur's neck-bone, which hung so low the head was no more than a foot off the ground. When the guard started shouting about the robbery, the boy had gotten up and skulked off, breaking into a run seconds later.

Bert followed him. Down the stairs they ran and through the aisles of the Hall of Reptiles and Amphibians. Bert chased the boy past display cases filled with snakes, alligators, and lizards mounted in their natural habitats.

"I want to talk to you!" Bert shouted. But the other boy merely looked over his shoulder and ran even faster, darting around a corner.

When Bert reached the turn, the red-headed boy was nowhere in sight. There were more rows of exhibits and at the end, a door marked MUSEUM PERSONNEL ONLY. KEEP OUT.

Bert walked up to the door and knocked. There was no answer. He tried the knob. It did not budge. The door was locked!

Puzzled and disappointed, he retraced his steps quickly. When he arrived in Dinosaur Hall, he nearly collided with the others, who were searching for him.

"Bert!" Freddie exclaimed. "Where have you been?"

"We've been looking all over for you," nine-year-old Scott Bishop added. "Finally, we came back in here, hoping you'd do the same."

Bert grinned. "That was a good idea." Then he told about the mysterious behavior of the redheaded boy. "He ran the minute he heard the guard yell. I thought that was suspicious."

"Did you catch him?" Flossie asked eagerly.

Bert shook his head. "The trail ended

at a locked door. Anyway, what about that robbery? What was stolen?"

"We don't know," Freddie replied. "The guard said it happened next door."

"Hmm. Must be in the Museum of History and Technology," Bert said. "That's where the special exhibit of commemorative stamps is. I really wanted to see that. I hope none of the stamps were taken."

"What's a commemorative stamp?" Flossie inquired.

"It's a stamp for a momentous occasion in history," Scott answered. "A commemorative stamp was made when the Panama Canal was built, and when we landed men on the moon. Sometimes a mistake is made in the printing and that makes the stamp even more interesting to collectors."

"What kind of a mistake?" Freddie asked.

"Well, when they printed a twenty-four-cent air mail stamp in 1918 some turned out with the airplane upside down."

Flossie giggled. "That's funny. Were they thrown away and were new ones made?"

"No. And now those stamps are very valuable. One of them is worth forty thousand dollars today because there are only a few left."

"Wow!" Freddie's eyes widened. "That's a fortune."

"Sure is," Scott agreed.

"You know a lot," Flossie remarked. She looked admiringly at the boy.

Scott grinned, a little embarrassed. "I collect stamps," he explained. "That's why I'm so interested in that special exhibit."

"Why don't we go there now?" Nan suggested. "We have some time before your mother picks us up."

"Good idea," Bert said.

"Tell me more about commem—those stamps," Flossie begged as Scott led the way to the Constitution Avenue entrance of the museum.

"Well, as I said, they are issued in honor of particular events and famous people—"

"I bet they made one for George Washington," Bert interrupted.

Flossie stopped in her tracks. "I know who George Washington is," she declared. "That's who was stolen!"

"What are you talking about?" Nan asked, staring at her sister in surprise.

"Well, when I followed that fat man, I heard him talking to another man just before he ran out the door. He said George Washington was gone!"

·2·

Puzzling Announcement

Bert, Nan, and Scott looked at Flossie in amazement.

"It sounds as if you've stumbled onto something, Floss!" Nan said. "Tell me who the fat man was talking with."

"I don't know," Flossie replied. "He was tall and thin and had gray hair. And his voice was a little like—like Mr. Corley's."

Nan grinned as she thought of her teacher. His voice was nasal and somewhat drawn out. He always seemed to be talking down to people.

"What did the man say?" She questioned her little sister. "And how did you manage to listen?"

"I slipped behind a pillar," Flossie said. "Skinny said to the fat man, 'What about George Washington?' Fatso told him that he was gone. Skinny asked where. Fatso started to answer, when they saw me peeking out from behind the column. They seemed upset and the fat man said, 'Beat it, kid.' Then they walked away real fast."

Nan frowned. "You should tell the police," she said.

"I will," Flossie said eagerly. "I see some officers right over there."

They had arrived at the door of the Museum of History and Technology. Several uniformed men were stopping people and telling them that the exhibit was temporarily closed.

"Oh, there's Lieutenant Michaels!" Scott exclaimed and pointed to a tall, black officer who seemed in charge. "He's a friend of Dad's. Let's talk to him."

The children approached the detective, who greeted Scott. "You come back tomorrow with your friends," he said. "Then you'll be able to see the stamps."

"But we have to talk to you," Scott insisted. "These are the Bobbsey twins, who have done a lot of detective work, and Flossie overheard something in the other building that might be important to this case!"

Officer Michaels smiled. "I've read about you children in the newspaper," he said. "Welcome to Washington. Now, which one is Flossie? Would you tell me what you heard?"

Flossie nodded and repeated her story.

The officer's face became serious. "We'll go inside," he decided. "Follow me." He waved one of his men aside and led the children into the museum toward the stamp exhibit.

"A case was broken into about an hour ago and a valuable stamp with the picture of George Washington was stolen," he told the children, pointing to a glass case.

"Wow!" Freddie exclaimed. "And nobody noticed?"

"The guard was distracted momentarily by an accomplice of the thief who staged a diversion," Officer Michaels went on. "Meanwhile, the glass was cut and the stamp was taken."

"Does the guard have any idea what the crooks looked like?" Bert inquired.

"Well, he saw a man running from the hall and chased him."

"Did he catch him?" Freddie asked eagerly.

"No, because as he was going out the door another guard accidentally got in his way. They collided and were thrown off balance. Meanwhile, the man escaped that way." Officer Michaels pointed in the direction of the Museum of Natural History, where the dinosaur was housed.

"That figures," Flossie said. "Was he a fat man in a brown suit?"

"Yes. He must be the man you overheard, Flossie. Tell me all about him, please. How did you happen to notice him?"

"Well, he was puffing as if he had been running," Flossie said. "And he knocked Freddie down. He was very rude and I followed him to tell him that, when he met the thin man at the door. And then he just disappeared in the crowd."

"Did you get a good look at his face?"

"Hmm," Flossie said. "He had small eyes, and he was almost bald, and he had a—a squashed nose, like this." She pressed her finger against her button nose, pressing it flat like a pancake.

Detective Michaels smiled and held out his hand. "Let me congratulate you, Flossie. You did a wonderful job of observation. You—"

Before he could finish speaking, another officer came in and waved to Lieutenant Michaels.

"Excuse me a minute," the friendly

policeman said. "I'll be right back."

While he was gone, the children looked around the room. There were many glass display cases with stamps, and Scott was about to walk over to one, when Flossie grabbed his sleeve and stopped him. "Wait," she whispered. "There he is!"

"There who is?" Nan asked.

"The man who knocked down Freddie."

All turned toward the stranger in a brown suit who had just come into the room through the door opposite to the street entrance. He was looking around nervously and heading for the entrance where the policemen were still sending away visitors.

"Let's tell Detective Michaels," Freddie whispered, and the youngsters hurried to the officer to report the news.

The tall policeman whirled, then nodded and darted toward the stranger.

"I'd like to speak to you, sir," he said,

flashing his identification.

"Why?" the heavyset man demanded. "I have a—"

He was interrupted by a guard who had come in after him. "He's the one!" the guard cried, rushing over to the group. "That's the man I chased! I lost him outside. But then he turned up again in the back of the building."

"And he's the one who ran into Freddie by the dinosaur and who said George Washington was missing!" Flossie blurted, her eyes wide.

"Now just a minute!" the stranger blustered. "What am I being accused of? I haven't done anything. And who are these kids?"

"Never mind," Detective Michaels cut him short. "I'm doing the questioning. What is your name, sir?"

"I believe I can answer all your questions, officer!" came a nasal, rather unpleasant voice from behind them. Everyone turned around to face a tall,

gray-haired man who wore expensive-looking clothes and carried a tightly rolled umbrella.

"I am Godfrey Tindall," he announced before the detective could ask anything. "I am the owner of the inverted George Washington stamp that some clever thief has stolen from under your very noses. Instead of browbeating this gentleman, you should be going about the business of finding the thief!"

"How did you get in here, Mr. Tindall?" Detective Michaels inquired.

"I have a pass from the museum that assures me entrance to all the buildings. You see, I am on the board of directors," Tindall informed him curtly.

The detective nodded. "Mr. Tindall, I'm John Michaels and I'm in charge of this case. We will make every effort to find your property."

The haughty stamp owner laughed unpleasantly. "You will, eh? I doubt you'll be able to trace a little piece of paper, about an inch square, in a small plastic block. My guess is that the thief by now is miles away from here. And I lost my favorite and valuable stamp for good!"

Detective Michaels took a deep breath. "Mr. Tindall," he said, "We have sealed off the museum. No one will leave without being searched. But things would move along faster if you would let me return to my interrogation of this man who was seen running away from the building."

To everyone but Flossie's great surprise, Mr. Tindall put his arm around the heavyset man.

"He was running because he was chasing the thief, my dear man," he declared. "He already told me. The offender was an Oriental in a black suit."

Officer Michaels frowned, taken aback by the announcement. "And you believe this man?" he challenged.

"I certainly do. He is my distinguished associate and friend Max Rothfield, one of the outstanding stamp and coin dealers in the country. He arranged this exhibit for me."

Flossie tugged on Nan's hand. "He's the skinny guy who talked to Mr. Rothfield by the door," she whispered.

Nan pressed her sister's shoulder as a sign that she had understood and motioned her to be quiet.

Mr. Tindall was now staring at the group of children. "And what is the kindergarten class doing in the middle of a police investigation?" he demanded. "Isn't that rather irregular?"

"No, it's not," Detective Michaels replied drily. "One of the children had also seen Mr. Rothfield running in the other building, and reported her suspicion to me. She is one of the Bobbsey twins, who are known for their ability to solve mysteries."

Tindall glared at Flossie. "Ah, yes, I remember seeing the child in the Dinosaur Hall, where Max informed me of the theft and told me about the man he chased. Too bad these brilliant young detectives don't have anything to offer regarding the thief!"

"Don't worry, we'll find him," the policeman assured the stamp collector. Nan had the feeling that it was a real effort for him to remain calm despite Mr. Tindall's infuriating attitude.

"I do hope so," the man drawled. "Mr. Rothfield will assist you as my personal representative. And," he added with a mean look at the twin detectives, "I would advise these children not to get in his way!"

A New Mystery

The younger twins recoiled at Mr. Tindall's harsh tone of voice, but not for long.

"We've solved lots of mysteries," Freddie spoke up staunchly. "Why don't you let us help?"

"I'll be glad to listen to anything you suggest," Lieutenant Michaels said kindly and winked at the children. "But I do believe you ought to leave now, since I have to talk to Mr. Rothfield. Scott, give my regards to your parents."

"I sure will," the boy said. He checked his wristwatch. "Oh boy! My mom was supposed to pick us up ten minutes ago. We'd better get going!" The Bobbseys followed him outside, where Mrs. Bishop was waiting in a green station wagon.

"Sorry we're late," Scott apologized. "But there was this burglary and Flossie overheard the two men who we think are involved in it talking and then we met Lieutenant Michaels and—"

"Whoa—slow down!" the blond-haired woman with the pretty face exclaimed as she opened the car door. "Get in first and then tell me everything from the beginning."

As soon as the children were settled and on the way to the Bishop home, they gave a full account of what had happened.

"As I see it," Mrs. Bishop said when they were finished, "Mr. Rothfield and Mr. Tindall really didn't do anything that contradicts their statement. Even the words Flossie overheard were on the level. Mr. Rothfield was chasing the thief and told Mr. Tindall that George Washington had disappeared."

"But then why did they seem so angry when they saw me listening behind the pillar?" Flossie piped up.

"Well, Mr. Tindall's valuable stamp had just been stolen. No wonder they were upset."

"But it's their attitude, Mom, that's so weird," Scott said. "I don't believe *one* word they said."

"Neither do I!" the four Bobbseys chorused.

"If I were Mr. Rothfield," Bert reasoned, "and I had taken the stamp, I wouldn't have gone back into the museum with it. Lieutenant Michaels said everyone would be searched, and I'm sure Rothfield expected that."

"We weren't searched," Scott pointed out.

"That's because you knew Lieutenant Michaels and he vouched for us," Bert said. "I still think Rothfield wouldn't have taken the chance."

"I agree," Nan said. "That means he must have gotten rid of the stamp before he went back into the museum."

"Aha!" Freddie beamed. "So you think Mr. Rothfield hid the stamp somewhere outside."

"Right!" Bert said. "We ought to go back and check!"

"Sounds good to me," Mrs. Bishop agreed. "But how about coming home for dinner first?"

"By that time the men could have removed the stamp," Bert insisted.

Scott's mother sighed deeply. "Well, suppose I take you back to the museum right now and pick you up in an hour? I have an errand to do anyway, and dinner can wait as long as you all aren't too hungry."

"Oh, we can wait to eat," Freddie said even though he was starved. Looking for the missing stamp was so much more important!

Mrs. Bishop returned to the Museum of Natural History and let the children out.

"Let's split up," Bert suggested as he closed the car door behind him. "You girls search here and we'll investigate the other building where the stamp collection is."

"Okay," Nan said. "We'll meet you here in one hour."

She took Flossie by the hand and the two walked off.

"Where do we look, Nan?" the little girl asked, bewildered by all the possibilities.

"First we'll walk around the museum and check out the wall, especially at ground level. Maybe the thief stuck the stamp by a corner and put a stone over it. Or he could have put it on a windowsill and covered it with something."

"Suppose he hid it in a car?" Flossie said.

"You can't park around here," Nan said. "And he didn't have time to go far.

Unless he had a helper, who was waiting for him in front of the museum with the engine running—"

She did not even want to imagine such a horrible thought. Instead, she resolutely pulled Flossie along. "Come on, we have to do the best we can."

A few minutes later, Flossie was turning over a large, flat stone next to the wall of the building. "Did you lose something, honey?" a passerby asked the little girl.

"Oh—uh—a piece of paper," Flossie stammered.

"It was probably blown away by the wind," the woman said and walked on.

Flossie stared after her. Then her eyes lighted on a tree with a ladder leaning against it. It led to a branch that seemed to have a hollow at the tip. Flossie stepped forward and looked at it. Maybe the thief hid the stamp in that hollow, she thought. She turned to tell Nan of her suspicion, but her sister had gone on and was disappearing around the corner of the building.

Quickly, Flossie summoned up her courage and climbed the ladder. It was a little wobbly, and when she reached the branch, she held on to it tightly and let out a deep breath. Then her hand felt around the hollow, but there was nothing inside!

Suddenly a voice boomed below her. "What are you doing up there?"

The words startled her and Flossie whirled around. At the foot of the ladder was a stony-faced man in overalls who carried a pair of clippers used for cutting hedges.

The abrupt movement made the ladder shake and Flossie felt it slip away from the tree. "I'm going to fall!" she gasped, then screamed at the top of her lungs.

The man below flung the clippers to the ground and held out his arms to catch the little girl. She crashed against him

hard, knocking him off his feet. Both tumbled on the soft grass. Neither of them was hurt. Still, the experience was so scary that Flossie began to cry.

"Now, now," the man tried to soothe her. "You'll be all right." He pulled Flossie to her feet and looked at her. "There. You see, not even a scratch."

But Flossie kept sobbing. She wiped away the tears with her hands, which had gotten dirty from the bark of the tree, and dark smudges soon covered her face.

It was then that Nan, wondering where her sister was, came back.

"Wha—what happened?" she stammered, seeing Flossie.

"The little tyke climbed up my ladder. I have no idea why," the gardener replied. "When I asked her what she was doing up there she lost her balance and fell. But I caught her and she's fine."

"Oh, thank you. Thank you very much," Nan said, bending over the small girl.

"I'm sure she meant no harm," the man said. "Even so, you should tell her not to climb ladders like that. She could have gotten hurt."

Nan nodded and tugged Flossie away from the tree. When both were out of sight of the gardener, Flossie stopped crying.

"I . . . I thought maybe the thief hid the stamp in the tree and you weren't around so I—"

"I understand, Floss," Nan said. "But you know that was a dangerous thing to do."

The little detective nodded sheepishly. "I know. I'm sorry."

"Let's just be thankful you didn't get hurt."

When the group met again in front of the station wagon, which had just pulled up, Mrs. Bishop did not have to ask whether the search had been successful. The unhappy faces of the children told her the answer.

"Nothing," Bert reported. "But I still want to come back tomorrow. We could've missed a clue somewhere."

Mrs. Bishop smiled thoughtfully. "And what happened to Flossie's face? It looks as if she fell into a barrel of mud!"

"No, she fell off a ladder," Nan said, sending a twinge through her sister. She explained what had happened. Then they discussed the theft until Mrs. Bishop pulled into the U-shaped driveway of a lovely brick home. Near the door stood a jolly-looking man with white hair that drooped into his eyes. He wore a bright-colored Hawaiian shirt, and when the children stepped out of the car, he held up both hands as if he were holding pistols.

"Stand and deliver!" he bellowed. "Mrs. Bishop, I'm hunting down the Bobbsey twins!"

"Who in the world is he?" Nan whispered to Scott. But before he could answer, the man walked over to them, his round tummy bouncing, and cried, "How would you like to take on an exciting case?"

"Mr. Kelly!" Scott laughed. "How did you know the Bobbseys were here?"

"Your father told me. He mentioned how good they are at finding things that are lost. So, kids, how's about helping me find a missing monster?"

·4·
The Green Monster

"A monster?" Flossie shrieked.

Mr. Kelly nodded. "It's green."

"And it walks on six legs and has daisies growing out of its ears!" Bert said jokingly. He knew that the good-natured man had been kidding.

"It's friendly nevertheless," Mr. Kelly grinned.

"Can we see it?" Freddie asked.

"Sure."

"Suppose we all go into the house and discuss it while I fix dinner," Mrs. Bishop suggested, and led the way into the kitchen. While Scott set the table, Mr. Kelly began to tell his story.

"You see, I own a pet shop and have all kinds of animals, including two wonderful iguanas."

"What's an ig-u-ana?" Flossie asked.

"A green lizard. Mine happen to be from Mexico. I took one down to the Natural History Museum to show a group of school children. Now and then I give short lectures and bring animals along to demonstrate."

"But what does that have to do with the monster?" Freddie pressed on.

"Well, iguanas are friendly little monsters, and the one I took escaped!"

Flossie giggled. "Did you carry him in your pocket?"

"No, he's too long for that—almost two and a half feet. Would you like to see his brother?"

"Oh boy, would we!" Freddie squealed and the others chimed in.

"Well, you'll have some time before dinner is ready," Mrs. Bishop declared. "Would you like to go now?"

"Yes, yes!" the children cried, and after quick glasses of lemonade, all piled into Mr. Kelly's delivery truck which was parked on the street.

When they reached the shop a few minutes later, the owner led the visitors through the front door. They were greeted by barks, meows, and the shrieking of birds. A lovely blue-green parrot perched on an open trapeze immediately attracted Flossie.

"Oh, he's bee-yoo-ti-ful!" the little girl exclaimed.

"Bee-yoo-ti-ful, bee-yoo-ti-ful!" the parrot repeated.

Flossie laughed. "You're not very modest," she told the bird. "But you *are* beautiful."

"That's Pancho," Mr. Kelly said. "He repeats everything you say so long as it isn't too lengthy. He has trouble with sentences but he can remember a few words at a time."

"That's Pancho!" the bird squawked.

The children were delighted as they followed Mr. Kelly to the other side of the shop.

"Here's the iguana," he said, pointing to a large glass aquarium. It was filled with earth, rocks, plants, and a piece of driftwood. Draped around it was the iguana, eyes closed, napping.

"He *is* green!" Freddie exclaimed. "If he were as big as a dinosaur, he'd really be a monster."

"He comes from an area of Mexico that has lots of bright green leaves," Mr. Kelly explained. "They provide a natural camouflage, or cover, for the iguana to hide in. But he also loves to come out sometimes and sun himself on a comfortable tree branch."

"He sure looks like a distant relative of the dinosaur," Nan said, "with that long body and tail with its scaly skin."

"Can he jump?" Freddie inquired, pointing to the screen on top of the aquarium.

"Sure, and he can squeeze through the tiniest opening. He has small bones," Mr. Kelly replied.

Just then the iguana opened his eyes, slithered up the side wall, and before anyone could stop him, slid through a small space under the screen.

"Look out!" Bert shouted, but it was too late. The iguana was streaking across the floor.

"Watch the door," Mr. Kelly told Scott. "The rest of us will form a line and close in on him and herd him back home."

The maneuver proved successful, but when the lizard returned to the aquarium, he made no effort to go in the way he had left. Instead, he darted back and forth nervously, flicking his red tongue.

Quietly, Flossie slipped behind him and opened the door. Bert, Nan, and Freddie moved in even closer on the scared animal, and a moment later the little iguana backed into the aquarium.

"Hooray!" Scott shouted. "We caught him!"

"That was a good idea, Flossie," Mr. Kelly praised the small girl.

"Good idea, good idea," Pancho echoed.

The children laughed, and Mr. Kelly said, "Well, you've now had a demonstration of what iguanas are like. It might help you if you decide to take on the job of finding my missing monster."

"We'll go to work on it tomorrow," Bert suggested. "Agreed, gang?"

"Agreed," his brother and sisters assured him.

"Good," Mr. Kelly said. "I have an appointment at the museum at eleven. Suppose I meet you there at ten?"

"Fine," Scott said. "But now I think we'd better head home for dinner."

"I'm going to drive you back in a minute," Mr. Kelly promised and went to check on a row of fish tanks.

Suddenly, Flossie, who was standing

next to Scott in front of Pancho's trapeze, nudged the older boy. "Somebody's watching us!" she whispered.

"What!"

"Behind that curtain," Flossie said. Her eyes darted toward a doorway where a curtain was drawn almost entirely across the frame.

Scott took her by the hand, walked to the curtain, and flung it open. Behind it lay a storage room, and a mournful-looking raccoon that sat motionless in a cage, staring at them.

Scott made a face. "The monster's a spy!" he teased Flossie. "He heard every word you said!"

Flossie bit her lip. She was sure someone else had been behind that curtain, but did not reply.

"Time to go!" Mr. Kelly called, drawing the children outside and into the truck.

"I still think someone was watching us," Flossie murmured as the engine started. "And it wasn't a raccoon!"

Scott merely shrugged.

When they pulled out of the driveway and into the street, Bert's eyes suddenly fastened on the building next door.

"Hey, look!" he said, pointing. Lettered on the front window were the words MAX ROTHFIELD. RARE STAMPS AND COINS.

"Do you know Mr. Rothfield?" Nan asked Mr. Kelly.

He shook his head. "I rarely see him. Why?"

"Oh, we met him today at the museum," Nan went on, but did not comment further. She felt she shouldn't mention her suspicions to the stamp dealer's neighbor as long as nothing had been proved.

After a delicious meal of shrimp and steak at the Bishops' home, the Bobbseys and Scott disappeared into the family room to plan their strategy for the following day.

"As I see it," Bert began, "we ought to split up in order to tackle both cases at once. Some of us should work on the missing stamp while the others hunt for Mr. Kelly's iguana."

"But what about the laughing dinosaur?" Freddie put in.

"What laughing dinosaur?" Bert answered.

"Oh, I forgot to tell you. While you were chasing that redheaded kid, the dinosaur laughed."

"Well, you know on Mondays it sings the 'Star-Spangled Banner.' Freddie, you're being silly."

The little boy pouted. "No, I'm not. And when we finish solving the other mysteries, I'm going to find out what the dinosaur was laughing at!"

"Sure, and we'll help you," Nan promised, tousling his blond curls.

"All right," Bert said. "Now let's get serious. We all agree that Max probably took the stamp, but we don't know why or where it is."

"Right," his listeners chorused.

"I just thought of something," Scott

spoke up. "It would be almost impossible for the thief to sell the stamp, because it's so rare and everyone knows about it. So the only thing he could do is hold it for ransom."

"You mean, like in a kidnapping?" Flossie said.

"Something like that," Scott agreed.

"Wait a minute," Nan said. "Suppose Mr. Tindall stole his own stamp, or had Max Rothfield steal it for him. He could claim the insurance money for it. Something expensive like that is bound to be insured, isn't it, Scott?"

"All valuable collections are insured," Scott confirmed.

"Hey, that's it! Nan, you're a genius!" Freddie whooped in excitement.

"Hold it," Bert said, raising a hand. "If Tindall wanted money, he could have sold the stamp. If he collects from the insurance company, he won't be able to sell the stolen stamp, so it would be worthless to him."

"Unless he wanted both the money

and the stamp," Scott concluded. "Collectors are very fond of their stamps and often don't want to get rid of them."

The doorbell suddenly interrupted, and Bert got up to see who it was. But when he opened the door, no one was outside. Instead, a piece of paper lay on the stoop. As he picked it up, he heard someone running away along the side of the house.

He brought the note inside and showed it to the others. "Someone left this message," he explained.

"What does it say?" Scott asked.

Bert opened it while everyone else looked over his shoulder. Printed in big, sloppy letters were the words:

BOBBSEY TWINS
BEWARE OF THE LAUGHING
DINOSAUR!

A Tricky Disappearance

"I knew it!" Freddie chirped. "You see, I told you. The dinosaur did laugh. This proves it."

Scott frowned as he took the note from Bert and examined it. "Pretty clever," he said. "Whoever sent it cut each letter out of a newspaper or magazine and pasted it on the paper."

"That's so we couldn't trace the handwriting," Bert declared, sending a shiver through Flossie.

"Someone's trying to scare us," she said. "He made that dinosaur laugh and now he's trying to scare us!"

"He could've wired up the dinosaur and laughed through a microphone out of sight," Nan said thoughtfully. "But why use that to scare us? There's nothing frightening about a laughing dinosaur!"

"That's right," Bert said. "So don't you worry about it, Floss. My guess is that it was just a harmless prank."

"Maybe it has something to do with the missing stamp," Freddie observed. "The first time we saw Max was right by the dinosaur, remember?"

Bert shrugged. "Let's hit the sack. Maybe we'll find a clue tomorrow."

An hour later Freddie was still tossing and turning in bed, while his brother slept soundly in the bunk above him. The little boy kept thinking about the dinosaur and the mysterious laughter. Then he wondered about the iguana and imagined it was prowling around the dark museum. At last, swallowing a yawn, he drifted off into a restless sleep.

Suddenly, Freddie found himself

walking through the museum. It was night, pitch-black, and the skeletons of dinosaurs rose his over head making his heart pump faster.

He tried to leave but every door was locked. He walked faster and faster, going nowhere. Then he heard a loud laugh that rumbled through the big halls. It sounded like a ghost's!

Freddie started to run. He heard footsteps pounding behind him. Something enormous was chasing him! He ran faster and looked back over his shoulder, seeing an iguana. But it wasn't small like the one in Mr. Kelly's pet shop. It was huge like a dinosaur. And it was running on its hind legs!

Freddie screamed as the dinosaur laughed, shooting its great, red tongue out of its mouth.

"Help!" Freddie wanted to cry, but the word caught in his mouth. He ran as fast as he could but the beast was gaining on him.

"Help!" Freddie finally shouted. Just

then the iguana's great clawed foot came down on him and threw him to the floor with a terrible crash.

"Freddie, what's the matter?" Bert sat up in his bunk and stared at his brother, who was lying on the bedroom carpet.

"Help!" Freddie cried. "The iguana's going to get me!"

Bert jumped down and put an arm around his little brother. "You've been dreaming," he said soothingly. "And you fell out of bed!"

Freddie opened his eyes, his heart still beating wildly. "I . . . I guess I was," he stammered. "And it was scary. A giant iguana was chasing me."

"It's all over now," Bert said. "Come on, let's go back to sleep."

"Can I sleep in your bed?" Freddie was a little embarrassed to ask, but the dream had been so real that he was afraid it would come back when he closed his eyes again.

"Sure," Bert said. "Come on up."

With Bert next to him, Freddie felt safer and soon both of them closed their eyes and slept.

The next morning, Mr. Bishop dropped the Bobbseys and Scott at the museum on his way to work. At ten o'clock sharp they were waiting in the lobby for Mr. Kelly, who arrived a few moments later.

"Hi, kids," he greeted them in his usual friendly way. "We'll have to hurry because I have quite a few things to do before I give my lecture today."

He led the way to a lower level and down a long corridor to a door marked MUSEUM PERSONNEL ONLY. A guard sat in front of it.

"That's the same sign that was on the door I saw yesterday," Bert commented. "And it was on this floor, too." He turned to the guard. "Is there another entrance to this room, sir?"

"Why yes," the man replied, pointing

in the direction where Bert had followed the redheaded boy the previous day. "It's at the other end of this room."

"Thank you," Bert said, trailing after Mr. Kelly and the others.

"Wait a minute, son," the guard called out. "Why did you want to know?

Bert explained, and the guard sighed. "We try to keep that door locked, but sometimes the workers forget and we have to chase people out who wander in."

Bert nodded and then hurried to catch up with the others.

"Over here," Mr. Kelly said, motioning toward a long table covered with sweaters and personal articles belonging to the museum workers. "That's where the school children sat when I showed them my monster."

Freddie and Flossie instantly dropped on their hands and knees and began looking under the table. They crawled in opposite directions. Suddenly, Flossie saw a small dinosaur's head peek out at her from behind a box. *And it laughed!*

"Ohhhh!" she yelled. "There's a live dinosaur under here!"

Just then, Freddie's face appeared after the dinosaur. "Fooled you." He grinned.

"What?" Flossie was confused.

"It was me who laughed," Freddie explained, and held up the plastic toy.

Flossie stuck her tongue out at him. "I'll get you for that, Freddie Bobbsey!"

Bert and Nan, who had witnessed the scene, broke out in a fit of laughter as the younger twins scrambled up from under the table.

"Okay," Mr. Kelly said, "enough pranks. Come on, I'd like you to meet some friends of mine."

He headed around a corner into a larger room where a group of workers were constructing a tree. Later it would be moved out into the museum to become part of an exhibit.

A few feet away, a dark-haired woman was mixing a brown, sticky-looking material in a big pot.

"This is Mrs. Rickle," Mr. Kelly said. "She's making chocolate pudding."

"Can I taste it?" Flossie asked.

The woman laughed. "Mr. Kelly's joking. This is a paste we use for making footprints. You see, we take an exact model of a dinosaur's foot, for instance, press it into the brown material, and when we pick it up, it leaves a footprint."

"Why do you do that?" Freddie asked.

"To make the exhibits more real-looking," Scott put in.

"That's right," Mrs. Rickle continued. "We make trees, landscapes, all kinds of things. Here, let me show you." She picked up a stick and spread some of the goo on a wide board.

"If we want to make stony ground, we

spread the paste thickly, like this. Then, we take pebbles and small rocks and sprinkle them on top."

Flossie grinned. "And then you put in the foot model and leave a print."

"Exactly," the woman said, smiling.

"I remember there were footprints around the dinosaur we saw yesterday," Nan remarked.

"One of them I had just replaced," Mrs. Rickle said. "It had cracked."

"I bet Freddie did it when the man knocked him down and he fell underneath the dinosaur," Flossie said.

Freddie looked away sheepishly. "I didn't notice."

"It wasn't your fault," the woman said. "And it's no big deal making a new one."

Flossie was pointing to the tree that was being built. "Do you think an iguana could hide in its branches?" she asked.

"Not for long," Mrs. Rickle said. "One bite of those plastic leaves and it would know the tree wasn't real."

"The children are going to help me look for my missing iguana," Mr. Kelly explained. "And now, gang, it's that time. You'd better get to work. If we don't find him today, I'm afraid we may never find him."

Immediately, the children spread out and began to search. Freddie saw a large pile of boxes stacked up against the wall at the far end of the room. "Let's look behind those," he said to Flossie, and the two walked over to the spot. Carefully, they began moving the boxes. Suddenly they heard a scratching noise on the other side!

"Shhh!" Freddie cautioned. "Did you hear that?"

"Something must be back there," Flossie decided. "Let's pull these boxes away."

She had hardly finished speaking when the cartons, piled higher than their heads, toppled down, bouncing over the twins.

"Help!" Freddie yelled as he disappeared under the cardboard.

"Nan!" Flossie cried.

Nan, Bert, and Scott ran over to help. They pulled the cartons off the small twins and Nan pulled Freddie to his feet, a worried look on her face.

"Are you all right?" she asked.

"I'm okay." He gasped. "But someone was behind there. I saw red hair when he pushed the boxes over."

Flossie shook her blond curls and nodded. "I saw him, too. Only from the back."

Bert put his finger to his lips to signal everybody to be quiet, then tiptoed around the back. He heard the sounds of footsteps going down an aisle behind a row of lockers. Then a door slammed.

Bert gave chase and soon came to the second door the guard had told him about. He flung it open and found himself in the Hall of Reptiles!

"This is the same door the boy went

through yesterday," Bert muttered to himself, and rushed past the reptile displays. But when he reached the end of the hall, the fugitive had slipped out of sight without a trace!

·6·

Ticklish Discovery

"I lost him for the second time," Bert reported when he had gone back to the others. "This kid is faster than a flash of lightning, and he sure knows his way around here."

"But was it that redheaded boy again?" Nan asked.

"I think so. Both Freddie and Flossie saw a flash of red hair. Who else could it be?"

Just then Mr. Kelly walked up to the group with a short, neat-looking man who wore glasses perched on the end of his nose.

"This is Dr. Williams," he said, then

introduced the Bobbseys and Scott. "Dr.
Williams will answer any questions you
have. I must go now and prepare my little show. See you later."

The children shook hands with Dr.
Williams and Bert asked, "Sir, have you
seen a redheaded boy around here in the
last two days?"

Dr. Williams looked surprised. "Why,
yes," he replied. "Is he a friend of
yours?"

"No," Bert said, "but we think he's
been up to some mischief. We'd like to
find him."

Dr. Williams nodded. "There was a little redhead around yesterday, who drew
a mustache on one of the dinosaurs. For-
tunately, he didn't use anything that we
couldn't wash off. But I'd like to find
him, too!"

"Maybe he stole Mr. Kelly's iguana,"
Flossie piped up.

"He certainly is a suspect," Scott declared.

Freddie had been staring at Dr. Williams and finally asked, "Are you a real doctor? I mean, can you cure tummy aches?"

The man smiled. "I'm a doctor of philosophy in paleontology. That's not the same as a medical doctor."

"What—what is it?" Freddie looked confused.

"It means I studied a long time, just like a doctor who cures tummy aches. But I studied fossils, like the dinosaurs you've seen here."

Flossie giggled. "You're an old bones doctor," she said.

"That's a good way of describing it," Dr. Williams agreed. "Now, is there anything else I can do for you?"

Bert shook his head. "We've searched everywhere, and the iguana isn't here. So we might as well go on."

Dr. Williams escorted the children to the door where the guard had sat earlier. "It was very nice meeting you," he said.

"And I hope you find the iguana some-where. Maybe he's hiding in one of the exhibition halls."

The children thanked him and walked off. "I have an idea," Bert said. "Suppose Flossie and I start looking for the missing stamp. We'll go next door where the stamp show is."

"I'd like that," Flossie said.

"Good. The rest of you stay here to look for the stamp *and* the iguana," Bert went on.

"All right," Nan replied. "Suppose we meet at the stamp exhibit at noon."

Bert and Flossie nodded and walked off. Nan suggested that her team begin to search the Hall of Reptiles, then move upstairs to the dinosaur display.

Nothing turned up among the reptile exhibits, and half an hour later the children went upstairs. Soon they stood in front of the dinosaur again, where Freddie had been knocked down the day before.

Nan was about to study the new footprint, when Freddie tugged on her arm. "Look," he whispered.

Bert and Flossie, meanwhile, had gone to the Museum of History and Technology.

"We pretty much covered the outside of the building yesterday," Bert said. "And the stamp didn't turn up. But I think Max might have hidden it somewhere in the display room right after he took it. Then he ran outside, pretending to chase the thief, so that if he was searched he wouldn't have the stamp on him."

"Hmm, I see," Flossie said. "If he did that, I'm sure he planned way ahead of time where he would hide it."

"That's for sure," Bert said, as they entered the building. "Now, Floss, if you were a crook, where would you have put the stamp?"

Flossie looked around, tapping her finger against her cheek. "Sometimes the best place to hide something is right out in the open. But that wouldn't be a good idea here, since there are only glass cases and nothing else."

"Let's check out the display where the stamp was last seen," Bert decided, leading his little sister to the case. The broken glass had been replaced, and there was a small notice inside explaining that the stamp had been stolen. But other stamps surrounded the sign.

"Did boys really wear those funny short pants in those days?" Flossie asked and pointed at a picture that was part of the display.

Bert grinned. "I guess so. And the girls wore long dresses."

"They look like old ladies," Flossie said. "I'm glad I don't have to wear clothes like that." Then she pulled her brother's hand. "Come on, now, we have to look for the missing stamp, Bert!"

"Don't talk so loud," her brother cautioned her.

Flossie looked surprised. "Why?"

"Because," Bert explained, "I don't want anyone to know we're detectives. This way we may be able to overhear something. It could have been an inside job, you know. Perhaps the thief bribed one of the workers."

"You are so *right!*" Flossie said in a low tone and nudged him. She signaled with her eyes that someone was standing right behind them. Casually, Bert turned halfway and realized it was a guard.

"Come on, Flossie," Bert said. "Let's look at other things." He pulled his sister away, feeling the eyes of the guard on his back. As they left the room, the boy was angry with himself for letting someone come up so close behind them. I should have noticed, he chided himself. Some detective I am.

"I bet he thinks we're crooks," Flossie

whispered. "He had a funny look on his face."

"I doubt it," Bert said. He led his sister through a deserted gallery into an adjoining anteroom. "But now we have to figure out what to do next. Suppose—" He stopped short, hearing voices and footsteps around the corner.

"Flossie! That sounds like Max Rothfield and Mr. Tindall. We have to find a place to hide!"

"Over there!" Flossie pointed to a packing box in a corner.

Bert grabbed her hand tightly and pulled her along. "Good. We'll hide inside."

As fast as they could, the children lifted the lid and jumped in. Then Bert lowered the cover gently. They found themselves lying on a soft layer of Styrofoam insulation. Some loose excelsior, a strawlike material used to protect things, tickled Flossie's nose.

"This looks like a quiet place," came

the voice of Godfrey Tindall. "No one will eavesdrop on us here. Now, Max, how could you possibly have lost that stamp?"

"I told you a thousand times," Max Rothfield whined. "I had it wrapped in my handkerchief. Somewhere between here and that dinosaur over in the other museum it fell out."

Flossie nudged Bert, excitement in her eyes. Bert motioned for her to lie still.

"You fool!" Godfrey Tindall snapped. "Did you have it when our friend Ken tripped the other guard who was chasing you?"

"Yeah, I had it then. I'm sure of it. I must have lost it outside or in the other museum."

"Well, have you looked?" Tindall demanded.

"Of course, I looked. I looked all over the grounds and in the mall entrance to the Museum of Natural History. Went right back to the Dinosaur Hall where I ran into that Bobbsey boy. Those kids, by the way, were there today, too. They're watching me. And so are the cops."

"So what, they can't prove a thing," Tindall said. "But you'd better find that stamp, Max. I didn't have you steal it just to get the insurance money, you know. I love that stamp. It's one of my prized possessions. Even if no one else knows I own it, I know."

"Godfrey, I—"

"You get it back for me!" Tindall snapped, cutting off Max. "And if you don't, I'll tell the police all about you and your crooked deals. And I can prove what I know. *You* can't prove I had anything to do with the stamp theft."

"I'll find it, don't worry!" Max tried to sound hopeful but did not succeed.

"Meet me at the usual place by five o'clock," Tindall said coldly. "If you don't have it by then, you'll go to jail. It's as simple as that."

Flossie, lying with her nose against the piece of excelsior that was sticking up, now felt a tickle she couldn't control. It was building up to a sneeze!

Frantically, she signaled Bert. He tried to help her by holding her nose, but it was too late.

"Kaaaa CHEW!"

·7·

Roy's Revelation

Godfrey and Max froze. "There's somebody in that box," Tindall hissed. "Get 'em!"

Before Bert and Flossie could jump out and run away, the two men grabbed them, quickly gagging the children with handkerchiefs so they could not cry for help. Then they bound Bert's and Flossie's hands behind their backs with string that was lying in a corner of the box.

"Put them back in the box," Tindall snarled. "We'll get rid of them later."

"How are you going to do that?" Rothfield wanted to know.

"Get Ken Wilson, the guard whom we bribed. He'll find a way. We paid him enough money. He can help us get them out of here."

"Those nosy kids," Max muttered angrily as he put the cover on the box. "I knew they were watching me."

"Well, we're going to put an end to it," Tindall declared. "Hurry up and find Wilson. I'll stay here with the box."

Bert and Flossie were huddled inside the huge carton. Flossie shivered against her brother, making him feel bad that he had put her in such danger. To cheer her up, he began to hum a tune.

Flossie giggled, letting Bert know that she was all right. The gag wasn't tight and she could breathe easily.

Finally, Bert fell silent. His mind was racing as he tried to get his hands out of the bonds. Would the men take the box away before Nan, Scott, and Freddie realized their companions were missing? Where were the others when he needed them so much?

Meanwhile, as Nan, Freddie, and Scott stood in Dinosaur Hall, Freddie was pointing excitedly. "Nan! He's there again!" he exclaimed, watching the stamp dealer sneak around the spot where he had knocked the boy down.

"Why don't we ask him some questions?" Freddie said, and walked up to the man.

"I suppose you haven't found the stamp yet, Mr. Rothfield," the little boy said.

Max Rothfield whirled around, his pudgy face turning beet-red.

"Didn't Mr. Tindall tell you to stay out of my way?" he blustered. "I'm his representative, and if you interfere with my work, I'll have you thrown out of this museum!"

"I don't think you have any reason to," Nan said coolly. "We haven't done anything that the museum authorities could object to. We're just trying to help Mr. Tindall recover his stamp. Perhaps if you told us what you know we could be of assistance to both of you."

"I don't need your help!" Max bellowed. He was nervous and began to perspire. Angrily, he pulled out a handkerchief and mopped his forehead. "I know what I'm doing!" he declared. "I'll have this case wrapped up in no time. Now stay away from me, understand?"

Threateningly, he shook his fist. Freddie, despite the fact that he was only six years old, jumped out protectively in front of his sister. "Don't you shake your fist at Nan!" he said. "You can't hit my sister!"

"Ah," Rothfield waved his hand disgustedly. "You little flea. Who said anything about hitting anybody? Go play in your sandbox and leave the detective work to the grown-ups."

With that, he turned and walked off. Every once in a while he looked back, to make sure the children were not behind him.

"We have to follow him," Scott whispered. "But we have to wait until he's out of sight!"

"As soon as he's walked out the door, we'll run over and peek out to see which direction he's going in," Nan said. "Then—"

"Ha, ha, ha, ha, ha!"

She was interrupted by the dinosaur, who was laughing loudly!

"I knew it! I knew it!" Freddie shrieked, but Nan paid no attention to him. Instead, she quickly ran to the other side of the large fossil.

A redheaded boy was crouched down behind the low-slung neck. He laughed again.

Nan tiptoed up to him and tapped him on the shoulder. The boy jumped up, letting a big grin spread across his freckled face. "Okay, Nan," he said. "You caught me. You're a smart girl."

"How do you know my name?" Nan asked in surprise.

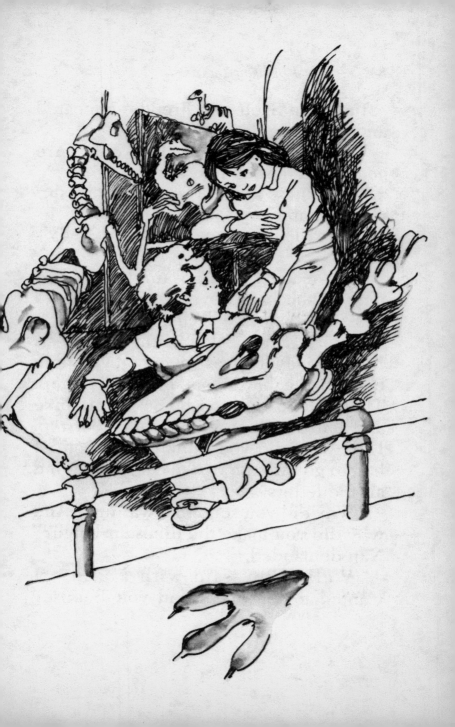

Just then Scott and Freddie appeared and ran up to them.

"Why, Roy!" Scott called out. "Are *you* the laughing dinosaur?"

"You know him?" Nan was more surprised than ever.

"Sure. This is Roy Kelly. Mr. Kelly's son."

"He made the dinosaur laugh, and pushed the boxes over on Freddie and Flossie!" Nan said accusingly.

"You're right," Roy said. "I confess. I'm the one who was spying on you from behind the curtain at my dad's shop. Then I followed you home on my bike and left the message on your doorstep. Hey, what did you think of that note? I had to go through two magazines to find all the letters."

"Why did you send that warning? And why did you make the dinosaur laugh?" Nan demanded.

"Well," Roy said with a grin, I wanted to see how good you Bobbsey twins really are. As detectives, I mean. I wanted to see if my dad was hiring the right people."

"You went to an awful lot of trouble to find that out," Nan said coolly. She was a little angry. "And you kept us from doing more important things because of your pranks!"

Roy's face fell. "Oh, don't be mad at me, please. I'm not a bad guy. Scott, tell her I'm not a bad guy, will you?"

"He isn't." Scott had to laugh. "But he loves to play jokes on people. When Bert mentioned a redheaded boy, I should have known it was Roy!" He slapped his forehead with his right hand.

"Well," Roy went on, "I had another reason for wanting to know how good you are." He sighed. "I need help. I'm in trouble."

"What kind of trouble?" Nan raised her eyebrows.

"Well," Roy said, looking at his feet, "I'm the one who took the iguana."

"What!" cried the Bobbseys and Scott.

"Why would you take him?" Freddie asked. "You can play with him every day in your dad's shop."

"Oh, I didn't steal him. That would be silly. I was just taking him to get some air in Potomac Park. But he squeezed out of the cage and got away."

"And you didn't tell your dad?" Freddie asked.

"No, I was too scared to tell him."

Freddie nodded. "Sometimes, when I do something wrong, I don't know how to tell my parents, either."

"It happens to everybody," Nan agreed. "But, Roy, you should tell him now."

"Well—could we hunt for the iguana first?" Roy looked pleadingly at the Bobbseys. "If we found him, it would make it a lot easier for me. And if we don't, well—then I'll tell Dad."

"Okay," Nan said. "But didn't you search for him already?"

"I did, but I didn't see him anywhere. Maybe if we all went after him we'd have a better chance. He got away in the park just a short distance from here."

"Aha!" said a booming voice behind them. "I see you've met my son." It was Mr. Kelly. Roy made a face that begged the children not to tell him the story.

"Have you found the iguana?" Mr. Kelly went on.

"No," Freddie said, "but we're going to look in—"

"We'll continue our search right after lunch," Nan interrupted, afraid that Freddie would reveal Roy's secret.

"Good," Mr. Kelly said. "I hope you find him. Roy, you be back at the shop by two o'clock to help me with the animals, will you?"

"Sure, Dad."

Mr. Kelly went off again, whistling.

"Thanks, gang," Roy said. "Now can we go to the park?"

"It's almost noon," Nan reminded

him. "And we were supposed to meet Bert and Flossie. Why don't you go to the park and wait for us? We'll be there as soon as we can."

They agreed on where they would meet, then Roy went out the Mall entrance toward the park while the Bobbseys and Scott walked to the Museum of History and Technology where the stamp exhibit was.

They sat down on the front steps and waited. But when Bert and Flossie didn't appear by twelve-thirty, Nan began to worry.

·8·

Trapped on Wheels

"This is very strange, very strange indeed," Nan said. "I think we ought to look for Bert and Flossie. Something must've happened."

Scott pinched his mouth tightly.

"Scott, you go left," the girl went on, "and Freddie and I will go right. We'll meet at the entrance at one. Okay?"

"Okay," Scott replied, and the children started their hunt. Nan and Freddie walked through one hall, then another and another, but found no sign of the missing twins.

"What'll we do, Nan?" Freddie asked worriedly.

"We'll go to the museum office and ask for help," Nan suggested.

"Wait!" Freddie whispered suddenly. "Look!"

He pointed to a doorway at the end of the hall. Max Rothfield was emerging. A security guard, who was pulling a board on wheels, was following him.

Nan and Freddie ducked behind a pillar as the pair went by.

"Hurry up, Wilson!" the stamp dealer panted. "We gotta get rid of those kids fast!"

"Yeah, yeah," the guard replied. "I'm coming. But I don't like this. It could cost me my job."

"Never mind, we're paying you plenty," Max hissed.

Nan and Freddie slipped out from behind the pillar and started to trail the men. They stayed back a good distance so they wouldn't be seen. Rothfield and

Wilson were completely unaware of the two young detectives and never looked back.

At last they rounded a corner, and Nan and Freddie stopped. When they peeked around the bend, they saw Godfrey Tindall helping the men tilt a large box onto the board with the wheels.

Nan nudged Freddie. "Maybe Bert and Flossie are in there!"

Freddie gulped in horror, as the men began to talk.

"All right, Wilson," Tindall said. "If you want your cut, see to it that Max gets this box with the kids out of here. Did you call for the truck?"

"Yeah," Max Rothfield replied. "He'll pull up to the delivery entrance in a few minutes. Listen, Godfrey, I don't like this. This is kidnapping!"

"So what?" Tindall said coldly. "Just do your job."

Around the corner, Nan grabbed Freddie's hand. "We have to help!" she whispered urgently. "You go and find a guard. I'll stay and watch the box."

"Okay," Freddie said, turning to leave. But as he did, he stumbled over a large ashtray filled with sand! He lost his balance and sprawled headlong on the floor!

"What's that?" Tindall yelled, and in a flash, all three men had rounded the corner. Before Nan and Freddie could recover, they were grabbed and subdued by the crooks, who muffled their shouts and carried them to the box! The children were quickly trussed and gagged and lifted into the box where the other twins lay. Bert's heart sank. He had been hoping that somehow Nan and Freddie would rescue them!

Tindall looked down at the Bobbseys and sneered. "Very snug, like four little sardines," he said. "That's what you get for poking your noses into matters that don't concern you."

He motioned to his partner, who low-

ered the lid. Then the children felt themselves moving. The box was being wheeled down the hall.

"I have to go now," they heard Tindall say. "Remember, find that stamp by five o'clock, Max, or else!"

The stamp dealer muttered something in reply that the Bobbseys couldn't understand. Then, except for the squeaking of wheels down the hall, there was silence.

The twins were squeezed tightly together in the box, but they were able to breathe without too much trouble. All four tried not to be too frightened as they thought of ways to escape.

Bert kicked his feet against the side of the box, hoping the noise would attract some attention. But the foam insulation was thick and the loose excelsior left little room to move.

Finally, as the box was wheeled down on an angle, Bert surmised it was a ramp. When they were on level ground again, he figured they were in the loading area at the back entrance to the museum.

An unfamiliar voice spoke now. "Hey, who are you, and what's in the box?"

"I'm Max Rothfield, Mr. Tindall's stamp dealer," the twins' captor replied. "I set up the exhibit for him."

"Oh, yes, Mr. Rothfield. But don't tell me you're taking the stamps out in such a huge carton."

Max tried a hearty laugh. "Oh, no. No, of course not. These are some things we don't need. I'm taking them away for other people to work with."

"All right. Is that your truck over there?"

"Yes, that's it."

"Good. Just load the box, then. I'll give you two a hand in a minute."

The Bobbseys were panic-stricken. If they were put on the truck, they might never be able to escape. Rothfield might take them to a desolate place and dump them where no one would ever find them!

Just then, Freddie brightened. If they

could all swing their bodies from side to side at the same time, they might turn the box over.

He nudged Bert, then tried to communicate the idea by moving back and forth as much as he could in a slow rhythm. Bert caught on immediately, and after a few more moments, they had alerted Nan and Flossie to their plan.

"One, two, three," Bert mumbled through his gag. Then all the children moved in unison, first to the left, then to the right. The box began to wobble!

"Hey!" called the guard who was in charge of the loading dock. "What in the world is in that box? It's moving."

"No, it isn't," Max Rothfield said, and put his hand on the carton to stop the rocking. "Grab hold here, Wilson."

But the guard was suspicious. "Wait a minute. Would you mind opening that crate?"

"Get him, Wilson!" Rothfield hissed, and before the startled dock guard knew what was happening, Wilson had knocked him down. "Run for the truck!" Max shouted, and both he and Ken Wilson sprinted toward the vehicle, jumped inside, and a moment later, roared off in a cloud of dust.

The guard, after regaining his feet, blew his whistle for help, then rushed to open the box. When he saw the four Bobbseys, tied up and gagged, he shouted, "I don't believe it! Who are you?"

He pulled off Bert's gag, and quickly got him a glass of water. Then, as Bert explained what happened, both untied the rest of the children.

"I'll call the police right away," the guard said. "You'd better come with me into my office, just in case anyone else comes around who wants you out of the way."

Fifteen minutes later, the Bobbseys were talking to Lieutenant Michaels and told him everything they had overheard while shadowing Rothfield and Tindall.

"Children," the detective said, "you've done an excellent job, much better than we were able to do. We were trailing the two men, but then had several emergencies so we lost them. There was a riot at a ball game for starters," he added, heaving a sigh. "But don't worry, we'll find Rothfield and Wilson and that truck of theirs. Did anyone get the license number?"

"I happened to look at it and I have a photographic memory," the dock guard offered. "It's YNG 667. The truck was a brown pickup." He gave the model as well.

"Excellent," Lieutenant Michaels said. "Now I think you children should go home and rest from your ordeal. One of my men can drive you."

"Thank you, but we have to meet Scott," Bert said. "He's waiting for us out front."

"Okay, but take it easy now, will you?

I don't want anything else to happen to my assistants!"

The children grinned, then waved good-bye to the men and ran outside. A few moments later they found Scott.

"It's about time," the boy said, frowning. "What happened to you?"

Excitedly, the young detectives told about their adventure. Scott's eyes opened wide. "Wait until Roy hears about this!" he cried.

"I hope he's still there," Nan said. "We're very late."

"Come on," Scott said. "We have to find him!"

·9·

A Slippery Catch

The children hurried out of the museum and headed for their meeting place in Potomac Park. Roy saw them coming and raced forward.

"I've been waiting and waiting," he complained.

Nan explained and Roy stood with his mouth open. "Boy, you *are* good detectives," he said admiringly. "Weren't you scared, though?"

"A little," Freddie admitted. "But it's all over now, so let's look for the iguana."

"I lost him right here," Roy said, "by

these rocks. It's a small area and I don't think he crossed the road with all the traffic. I hope he's still hiding somewhere in these rocks or trees. He loves trees."

"Let's divide up again," Bert said. "Roy, you—"

He was interrupted by a shout from the roadway. It was Detective Michaels. All the children ran over to him.

"Did you catch Godfrey and Max yet?" Bert asked eagerly.

"No. But it's just a matter of time. However, we found out that Godfrey Tindall not only tried to collect the insurance money; he did the same thing once before. He's wanted in London."

"What about the stamp?" Freddie inquired. "Has it been found yet?"

Sadly, Detective Michaels shook his head. "No, and we may never find it. Max could have dropped it anywhere outside and the wind could have blown it away. Unless he didn't tell Tindall the truth and stole it himself!"

"Well, we won't give up, sir," Freddie said staunchly. "We'll keep looking for it."

"I don't doubt it," the lieutenant said with a smile.

After he had driven off, Bert took charge again. "Freddie and Flossie, you look that way, over toward the cherry trees. Roy and I will cover the rocks."

The children searched and searched, but an hour later they still hadn't found anything.

"Do you realize we had no lunch today?" Freddie spoke up when they all met again. "I'm starved."

"Everybody's hungry," Nan said. "There's a hot dog stand on the road. Why don't you and Scott get something for us?"

"I'd love to!" Freddie said as Nan gave him the money.

A few minutes later, they all sat under a tree and began to eat with enthusiasm.

"Roy," Nan asked, "What do iguanas eat?"

"No meat," he replied. "They're strict vegetarians. At least the green ones are. There are black iguanas, too. I don't know what they eat."

Nan shrugged. "Too bad. I was hoping we could bait him with a hot dog."

"Not this one," Roy said. "He wouldn't eat it."

At the same moment, something dropped out of the cherry tree and landed on Flossie's shoulder. "Eeeeeech!" she shrieked. "It's—it's the iguana!"

Everyone was too startled to speak at first, but then Roy whispered, "Flossie, sit very still. Don't scare him away. Nan, can you grab him? You're right next to him."

Before Nan could reply, the iguana walked along Flossie's arm and straight up to the hot dog she was holding in her hand. Turning to blink at her once, he bit right into it!

"He ate it!" Freddie cried out. But as he did, the little green lizard extended his tongue disgustedly and let the piece of meat fall out.

"I told you he didn't like meat." Roy chuckled. "Now grab him, Nan, before he gets away again."

Nan moved her hand slowly and prepared to seize the iguana. But as soon as she wrapped her fingers around him, he squirted away like a bar of wet soap.

"Get him!" the children shouted as the lizard scooted off as fast as he could go.

Freddie and Flossie collided and went head over heels in the grass, laughing. Roy cut sharply in front of Scott, trying to grab the animal's trail, and tripped over his friend's feet. Both went down, too.

But Bert and Nan managed to corner the lizard and forced him to climb a cherry tree.

Roy had left the iguana's carrying cage in a rock crevasse when the lizard had escaped the first time, and now ran to retrieve it.

"Everyone form a circle around the tree," he said. "I'll climb up and get him."

To the children's surprise, the iguana, which was now perched on a low branch, did not move when Roy approached him. The boy was able to pick him up gently and put him in the cage without any trouble.

"Poor little iguana," Flossie said. "He must be hungry and scared." She rubbed her fingers sympathetically against the animal's nose. He blinked back at her through the bars.

Wearily, the little group made its way back to the museum. Mr. Kelly was still there, and Roy hurried to his father, beaming happily.

"We found him, Dad! He dropped out of a tree right on Flossie's arm." The boy explained how they had cornered the iguana and that he had been the one who took the animal into the park.

Mr. Kelly rumpled his son's hair. "No harm done. I just wish you had told me from the start. We could have looked in the park yesterday."

Roy swayed on his heels uneasily. "I know, Dad. I should've told you right away. I won't do it again."

"Good. Now, how about helping me load the animals I brought here today? Then I'll give you all a ride home."

When everybody was in the truck, Mr. Kelly asked, "How many of you want to go to the shop and put away Iggy here, then have a chicken and rib dinner at the Kelly homestead?"

"I do!" the children chorused.

"Good," Mr. Kelly said. "I'll call Mrs. Bishop to get her permission."

She didn't object and when Mr. Kelly had finished checking on all the animals, he said, "Well, that's it for today. Shop's closed. So let's go. Our house is next door."

"Oh, please," Flossie begged, "may I watch the animals for a little while?"

"Me, too!" Freddie chimed in. "We won't touch any of them. We just want to look at them."

Mr. Kelly hesitated, then his face lit in a smile. "Oh, why not? I'll show you how to lock up when you leave. It's very simple. You just turn the latch. We'll call you on this telephone when dinner's ready, so please answer it when it rings."

When Mr. Kelly and the older children had left, Freddie and Flossie grinned at each other.

"This is fun," Flossie said. "Now we have all the animals to ourselves."

"It's like being in a toy store," Freddie said. "Only the toys are alive!"

For almost thirty minutes, the twins roamed from cage to cage, watching and talking to the fishes, the lemur, and a curious creature, who was fat and furry, called a wombat. There were also dogs and cats and many birds besides Pancho the parrot.

"I wonder if that raccoon is still in the storeroom," Flossie commented and went to the curtain. But when she parted it, she froze in terror.

Behind the drape stood Max Rothfield!

For an instant, neither of the young detectives was able to move. Then, Flossie whispered, "Run, Freddie!"

But it was too late.

10

Pancho's Help

The crooked stamp dealer grabbed Flossie and Freddie by the arms and pulled them behind the curtain.

"One peep out of you kids and I'll make you wish you were never born!" he growled.

The twins stared at him. Then Freddie squared his shoulders. "Don't worry," he said. "We won't yell. How did you get into Mr. Kelly's shop?"

"Never mind. Just keep quiet," Max Rothfield said, holding onto them tightly. He thought for a moment, then went on, "I'm a desperate man, you understand. I'm running from the police, and it's your fault. If you hadn't been so nosy, none of this would have happened. Now you're going to be my hostages!"

"What're hostages?" Flossie asked, her lips quivering.

"They're people who hold you until they get what they want. And if they don't get it, they finish you off! Understand?" Rothfield said coldly.

Flossie began to cry.

"Keep quiet!" the man snapped at her. "I told you, no noise." He dragged the twins to a back door with a window at the top. "See that police car out there? There's another one down the street. Your friend, Detective Michaels, and his cops are waiting for me to come out of my store. When they get tired of waiting, they'll go in and look for me. That's when I'll make my break—and I'll take you with me!"

"But how did you get in here?" Freddie asked, trying to keep calm and think like a detective.

"I went to my shop before the cops

came," Max said. "Wanted to get my money and some of my more valuable coins and stamps." He pointed to a suitcase that stood on the floor some distance away. "But before I could leave, the law arrived. So I went across the roof and down the fire escape and through the back door. Mr. Kelly is careless about locking it."

"What about Mr. Tindall?" Flossie piped up.

"He ran out on me. He's on his way to South America. I hope the cops catch him, that rat. He left me to take all the blame. Now quit asking so many questions."

Suddenly, the phone rang. Max jumped nervously, but he did not release his grip on the children.

"Mr. Rothfield," Freddie said, "that's Mr. Kelly. If we don't answer, he'll come over here to look for us."

"That's fine with me," Max replied, an evil smirk on his face. "I need the keys to his truck!"

The phone stopped ringing, and a few moments later the front door opened.

"Freddie, Flossie!" Mr. Kelly called out. "Where are you?"

The twins could not reply, since Max had clapped his hands over their mouths. Then the curtain swung open and Mr. Kelly stood before them. When he saw Max Rothfield holding the children, his face contorted with anger.

"What do you think you're doing?" he thundered.

"Don't step any closer!" Max rasped, twisting one hand in his pocket as if there was a weapon inside. "I wouldn't hesitate to use this."

Mr. Kelly wasn't sure whether the man was bluffing or not, but he could not take a chance.

"What do you want?" he asked.

"Go outside and get your truck. Drive it up next to this side door. Then you stay there until I come out with the kids."

"You won't get away with this, Max," Mr. Kelly said. "Let the kids go and I'll

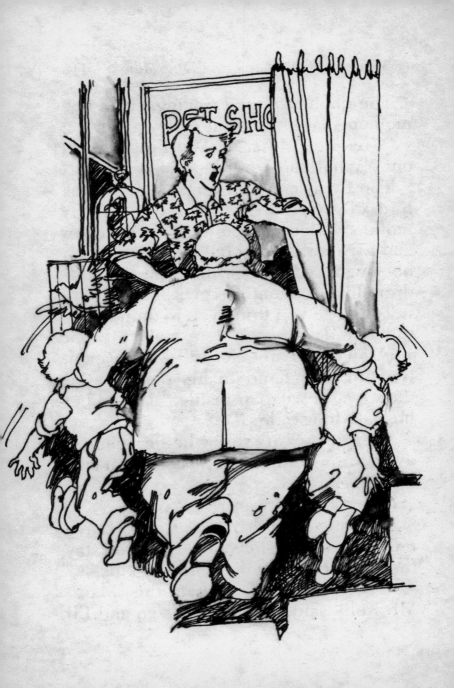

drive you anywhere you want. To the airport, anywhere—"

"Stay where you are!" Max shouted, his big, thick hands now around the children's necks. "I'm going to squeeze until you get that truck."

Mr. Kelly bit his lip. "Don't worry, children, you'll be all right. I'll do as he says." He turned and left the shop. Within a minute he had driven up to the side door.

Max released his hold on the children and shoved them into a corner. "Now stay there until I grab my suitcase," he said.

He walked toward his bag when Freddie realized that he and Flossie were standing next to a covered bird cage. Through a crack he could see Pancho.

The little detective's mind raced. He was convinced that Max Rothfield was bluffing and didn't have a weapon. Otherwise, he would have drawn it to make sure the children didn't move. Instead, Max was turning his back to pick up the suitcase.

At the same moment, Freddie pulled the cover off the cage and whispered to the parrot, "Stick 'em up, Max!"

Pancho, ruffling his feathers, stretched his neck and repeated the words. "Stick 'em up, Max!" he screeched.

Rothfield jumped in fright. Then he raised his hands high. "Don't shoot, don't shoot!" he pleaded.

Freddie grabbed Flossie's hand and pulled her to the side entrance. "Mr. Rothfield was only bluffing," he yelled. "Run!"

When the two dashed out the door, Mr. Kelly, who had heard Freddie's words, leaped out of the truck, and together with the children, dashed across the street to the police car. "Max Rothfield is in the pet shop!" he called out to Lieutenant Michaels.

"And Tindall is trying to get on a plane

to South America," Freddie added.

"I know," the policeman replied. "My men just picked him up at the airport. Is Max armed?"

"He said he was, but he was bluffing," Flossie declared.

Detective Michaels picked up a bullhorn and called to the stamp dealer. "Come out, Rothfield. You can't get away. Come out with your hands up."

Nothing happened for a moment, but finally Max Rothfield appeared, his hands clasped over his head. The lieutenant and two other policemen rushed forward and snapped handcuffs on him.

Rothfield looked beaten. "Did you get that rat Tindall?" he asked.

"Yes," Detective Michaels replied.

"I'm glad. I'll testify against him in court," the prisoner muttered.

"We'll appreciate that," Lieutenant Michaels said briskly.

In the same instant, attracted by the

commotion, Nan, Bert, Scott, and Roy came running out of the Kellys' house. Seeing the captive, they gaped in surprise.

"Looks like we missed out on all the excitement," Nan said, casting a worried glance at Freddie and Flossie.

"We're okay, Nan," Flossie assured her. "Mr. Rothfield was going to take us with him as hos . . . hostages, but then he got caught because Pancho told him to stick ' em up!"

"Pancho? Now wait a minute!" Bert broke in. "You'd better start from the beginning."

The children did, and Lieutenant Michaels shook his head in disbelief. "You kids put my whole police department to shame," he said. "I've never seen anything like this."

"Sir," Bert said, "when you book Mr. Rothfield, would you ask him exactly where he went from the time he stole the stamp until he found it missing?"

The detective looked at the crooked dealer. "You know that you don't have to answer any questions without talking to your attorney first," he stated. "But if you want to cooperate—"

Rothfield looked craftily at the detective. "Oh, I'll tell you," he said, "when we get to headquarters. But only on one condition!"

11

Footprint Find

"What is that condition?" Lieutenant Michaels demanded.

"That the Bobbseys drop the kidnapping charge."

"All right," Bert said. "We just want to finish up the case."

The detective turned to the children.

"Drop by headquarters in the morning. I'll have the information for you then. But I must warn you. My men have been over every inch of ground in and around the museum and have come up empty-handed. I don't think you're ever going to find that stamp."

Bert nodded, then the children said good-bye to Lieutenant Michaels, and Mr. Kelly took them home for their delayed dinner.

Next morning, after breakfast at the Bishops' house, the twins and Scott went to the police station to pick up the transcript of what Max Rothfield had told the police. Roy went along too, after promising his father that he would do his chores later.

"I know you kids are good detectives," Roy said on the way to the museum. "But do you really think you can find that stamp?"

Bert shrugged. "All we can do is try once more."

When they arrived, they studied the course Max Rothfield had taken and again searched the grounds between the Museum of Natural History and the Museum of History and Technology, then the halls of each one.

The door that the stamp dealer had

gone through proved to be the same one that Roy had used when Bert chased him.

"I guess it was open, until Roy locked it to keep me out," Bert reasoned.

"You're right. It was open," Roy confirmed.

Nan, meanwhile, was looking at the transcript. "It says here that Max had planned to hand the stamp to Mr. Tindall, who was supposed to meet him outside of the museum. But they didn't get their timing straight, so Max just kept the stamp and ran. He came down here into the workroom, because he thought he could put the stamp in one of the lockers. But there were too many people around."

"So he just kept running and ended up in Dinosaur Hall," Freddie said.

"Exactly," Nan replied. "He says he remembers running past some brown stuff. That's what he calls the goo they use for landscaping the exhibits. Then he got to the dinosaur and found the stamp missing."

"Wait a minute!" Bert said. "Suppose that stamp fell out of his handkerchief and wound up in Mrs. Rickle's goo pot?"

"Yes," Freddie cried, his eyes shining. "We've looked everywhere else."

The youngsters approached Mrs. Rickle and told her their deduction.

"Oh, dear, I'm afraid I won't be able to help you with that," the woman said. "I emptied the pot last night and cleaned it."

"Oh!" Nan's face fell.

"Wait," Freddie spoke up. "Mrs. Rickle, you told us yesterday that you replaced a footprint for the dinosaur upstairs after I fell on it, right?"

"Right. I had a lot of paste ready, and when the guard reported that the old footprint was damaged, I went up and made a new one."

"Then maybe the stamp did fall in the pot and was mixed up and got buried in the print!" Freddie declared.

Nan stared at Mrs. Rickle. "Do you think that's possible?" she asked.

The museum worker shrugged. "I suppose it would be possible," she replied.

"Let's go look at the footprint," Freddie said.

"Mrs. Rickle, if we have to break it in order to see if the stamp is inside, do we have permission?"

The woman smiled. "I'll be glad to make another one in order to help you solve the mystery," she said.

"Whoopee!" Freddie shouted and ran ahead of the others into the hall of the dinosaurs. The others followed.

"It's really a far-out idea," Nan said to Bert. "And yet, we've looked everywhere else!"

When the children arrived at the laughing dinosaur, Freddie ran his hand

over the surface of the new footprint. Suddenly he let out a squeal.

"Look!" he shouted. "Right here. Feel this sharp thing sticking up? I bet it's a corner of the plastic shield they put around the George Washington stamp."

Bert took out his scout knife. "Let me see, Freddie," he asked, and bent down. Carefully he scraped away the brown material from the sharp corner. In a few minutes he had removed enough to be sure.

"We found it!" he cried "It *is* the missing stamp!" With a few more moves of his knife, Bert freed the small, plastic container.

"What!" a voice suddenly boomed behind them. "You mean you really found it?"

The children whirled to face Detective Michaels.

"Yes, we did," Flossie chirped. "The dinosaur was almost stepping on it the whole time!" she giggled.

"That's wonderful!" Lieutenant Michaels said. "You have done an invaluable service to the museum and the police department!"

"Now all that's missing is the crooked guard," Nan said. "Ken Wilson."

"We rounded him up a little while ago," the policeman informed them. "He admitted everything."

"Hooray! The case is solved!" Freddie exclaimed, jumping high in the air. He had no idea that he would soon be trying to figure out another one called *The Music Box Mystery*.

Suddenly, there was a noise behind them. "Ha-ha-ha-ha-ha!" the dinosaur roared gleefully, while Roy stayed carefully hidden.